Cock-a-Moo-Moo

For Tony, Amelia, Alexander, and Theo — J. D-C.

To my auntie, Madeleine — you're a star! — A. B.

ISBN 0-439-60724-8

12 11 10 9 8 7 6 5 4 3   4 5 6 7 8 9/0

Printed in the U.S.A.   40

First Scholastic printing, March 2004

Cock-a-Moo-Moo

by Juliet Dallas-Conté

illustrated by Alison Bartlett

SCHOLASTIC INC.
New York   Toronto   London   Auckland   Sydney
Mexico City   New Delhi   Hong Kong   Buenos Aires

Poor Rooster had forgotten how to crow.

When the sun came up in the
morning, he took a deep breath
and shouted . . .

"COCK-A-MOO-MOO!"

"That's not right!"
said the cows.
"Only cows go moo."

So he tried again.

"COCK-A-

QUACK-QUACK!"

"That's not right!" said the ducks.
"Only ducks go quack."

So he tried again.

"Silly Rooster!"
said the chickens.
"You're getting it all wrong."

Rooster was very unhappy. "I'm never going to crow again," he said.

But that night, when all the animals were asleep, Rooster heard a noise.

Someone was sniffing . . .
and rustling . . . and sneaking
into the henhouse! It was a . . .

FOX!

"COCK-A-MOO-MOO!" shouted Rooster. "COCK-A-QUACK-QUACK! COCK-A-OINK-OINK! COCK-A-BAA-BAA!"

All the animals woke up!

They came running and chased the fox away.

"We're saved," clucked the chickens.
"You're a hero!" cried all the animals.
Rooster was so happy.

"COCK-A-DOODLE-DOO!"

he crowed.

And he never got it wrong again.